—THE—
CHINA RUN

BEING THE BIOGRAPHY OF A GREAT-GRANDMOTHER

NEIL PATERSON

RICHARD DREW PUBLISHING

Glasgow

First published 1948
by Hodder & Stoughton

This edition first published 1986
by Richard Drew Publishing Ltd.,
6 Clairmont Gardens, Glasgow G3 7LW,
Scotland

British Library Cataloguing in Publication Data

Paterson, Neil
  The China Run – (Scottish Collection)
  I. Title   II. Series
  823'.914 [F]   PR6066.A875/

  ISBN 0-86267-147-7
  ISBN 0-86267-146-9 Pbk

The publisher acknowledges the
financial assistance of the
Scottish Arts Council
in the publication of this book.

Printed in Great Britain by
Blantyre Printing & Binding Co. Ltd.

TO
MY FATHER

I

I HAVE two portraits of her. One shows a young woman in gay apparel against a back-ground of richly brocaded drapes. The gown is purple and of satin. It is cut low at the neck and is clasped to her waist by a wide bejewelled sash, while on her head, Arab fashion, is a scarlet shawl embroidered with white camels. She is standing with a hand on her hip and one cheek, so to speak, raised. It is a full-length portrait and you cannot see the face clearly. You can see, however, that the eyes are astonishingly blue and that the mouth is too large and wide, that the face is oval and is crowned, presumably, by red-brown hair, a tendril of which protrudes from the shawl in a small perfect curl, plumb centre and so meticulous that it fails altogether in its artistic aim of happy mischance and sits on the smooth, broad forehead with an air of grotesque permanency, rather like the tail on a piglet's bottom. The stance, the tilt of the head, the brassy stare, and of course the dress are, to say the least of it, provocative, and I cannot but think that her neighbours in old Banff must have found it all very shocking. Even I, in this day of grace and enlightenment, prejudiced as I am in her favour, cannot honestly claim that she looks like a Burgess of Banff, for in fact of course she does not look like a woman from our part of the coast at all: she does not look respectable.

The other portrait was painted some thirty years later and provides a measure of redress. The artist was John Ogilvie, of Banff, who was justly renowned for his taste, and he has certainly made a discreet job of her. She is sitting in a high-backed chair—Chippendale probably, but you cannot see the legs as the portrait ends in the region of the lap—and for background there is a cream wall decorated with a copper warming-pan, three etchings, and a Nanking chop-bowl. She is dressed to conceal. Black closets her throat and wrists and primly envelops the upperworks—no definite or undulating lines—so that the vulgar details of figure are quite obscured and your attention, consequently, must focus where it ought : on the face. It has not a great deal of character, this face. The forehead and jaw are good. The mouth, obviously painted with care, is firm and large and, I like to think, faintly humorous. The eyes are still startlingly blue, and every surrounding wrinkle has been copied, you feel, with painstaking attention to the original. You have no doubt that this is a photographic facsimile of the sitter, yet the result is oddly impersonal. It is the face of any peasant, on the brink of old age.

When you look from the earlier anonymous portrait to this fine painting of John Ogilvie's in its ornate, expensive frame, you realize immediately that this is a solid work of art, a proper portrait, an article which any ancestor would be proud to hang on his parlour wall; and you realize also, I think, that a hundred years ago a woman did not have a lot of fun, or if she did she had it for a short time only.

9

For a time I had both portraits hung in prominent positions, the young woman in my hall and the middle-aged one in my dining-room, but, to be candid, they palled on me, and after a month or two I shifted them to the top of the stairs where they are not quite so noticeable. They now hang side by side, and if you are interested in this sort of thing you have an excellent opportunity of studying them for points in common. Personally, I can find only two. They are both in oils, and neither does her justice.

2

Little is known of her early life, and what is known is easily told. She was born in 1829 in a two-roomed house in Carmelite Street in the Royal and Ancient Burgh of Banff, and was baptized later the same year in the name of Christian West. Her father was Alexander West, erstwhile stay-maker and, at the time of Christian's birth, town missionary with a stipend of 16 bolls bear, 8 bolls meal, and £21 10s. 5½d. in money. Her mother's name was

Jannet West or Gordon, and that is all that I can learn of her, although I have no doubt that she was a dutiful wife and a good mother. She was certainly a housekeeper of parts, for it has been recorded that the West family fared well and did not go without: an achievement you honour when you count the bodies she clothed and the mouths she fed: nine, including her own.

The family consisted of Alexander, the eldest son who went to sea at eleven, deserted his ship in Valparaiso and was never heard of again; Janet (note the modern spelling), Bathia, Elspet, Jean and Christian, daughters in that order; and finally, and somewhat unexpectedly, one imagines, as he arrived in his mother's forty-eighth year, Robbie, the puir laddie that was born stunted. In addition there were two sons who died in infancy and whose names, William and George, you may find on the family stone. And, naturally enough in so long and fruitful a marriage, there were others also, but they did not come to anything and, not having been christened, were disposed of without pomp or record.

No one appears to have noticed anything remarkable about the young Christian West, and one is forced to the conclusion that, as a child, she may have seemed as amiable, as estimable, and as dull as her sisters who, apart possibly from Janet who held a brief appointment as mistress at the Madras School, were, I think, very dull dogs indeed. They never learned to read or write. They failed to land husbands, and they could not even make a decent job of their needlework. They were myopic. They were failures. None of them, Christian included, ever went to school. There was, of course, no school for girls in those days, and even Young Ladies, as distinct from girls, had to be sent abroad, sometimes as far as Aberdeen, fortysix miles distant, to be educated. I am puzzled, accordingly, to account for Christian's education. One does not learn to read, write extraordinarily well, and to quote Latin at Sunday school, one has better things to do. The only explanation that I can offer is that her father, a scholar though a humble man, somehow found the time and place to instruct her. If this is so he must surely have got some inkling of her quality, and it becomes more surprising than ever that he did not boost her talents or show any sign of pride in her precocity. No doubt his wife persuaded him to keep it quiet. After all, it is not every hedge-sparrow that likes to have a cuckoo in the nest. They are too hard to dispose of.

At the age of sixteen Christian, unhandicapped by any reputation for brains, reached woman's estate, and promptly married. To the chronicler this marriage of Christian's is like the parting of a heavy curtain, for there is now an end to obscurity. We are done with supposition and guesswork. The panorama is of fact and, as incident jostles incident to reach the pen, men and women emerge clean-cut and complete from the shadows and voices clamour to be heard. It is a turbulent vista.

3

In the autumn of 1845 a strange ship, running before a south-easterly gale, rounded Kinnaird Head and, slipping into Banff Bay for shelter under the lee of the land, dropped anchor. She was a big ship for the bay, square-rigged and heavily sparred, black, lean-bodied, sinister, built for speed. It was rumoured she was an opium runner and curiosity rustled through the town. People collected on the foreshore and on the braes to study her, and the following morning when word got about that the captain's gig was being lowered a crowd quickly gathered on the New Harbour Wall.

It was an inquisitive and eager crowd, a hotchpotch cross-section of the town, with the girls and tradesmen to the front. The five West girls were there, arms linked, agiggle, and when Captain Dai Evans, ascending the iron rungs, poked his dark head over the edge of the quay, it is possible that the first sight that met his eyes was the row of crinolined Sunday skirts belonging to the Wests. He noticed Christian immediately, as well he might with her sisters to offset her, and a look passed between them. For a moment it seemed that he might speak, but, according to his own account, " becoming mindful of the proprieties" he gathered himself and proceeded on his occasions, namely a visit to the Black Bull Inn, where he knocked back two pints of strong ale, gave out that he was bound for Aberdeen with a cargo of tea and a badly sprung mainmast, and, after demanding the names of a reputable builder and a chandler, made discreet enquiries of the five sisters.

Later that gusty day he encountered them in full sail in Bridge Street, and his interest on that occasion was so marked that the whole town heard of it. When they had passed he swivelled in his tracks and watched them till they rounded the bend into Reid Street.

" A trim ship," he said. " And she looks to be running free."

For two unnecessary days—for his sprung mast was quickly unshipped and a jury fitted—he stayed on at the Black Bull, probing the locals in a subtle Welsh way for information anent the Wests and unaware that the town buzzed with it. On the third day the wind was so fair that it could no longer be disregarded and, abandoning his caution, he sought an interview of Alexander West. Inns, naturally, were out of bounds to the missionary, and so the meeting took place in the little house across the way from the burial-ground. The living-room was cleared for the occasion and the women retired to ' the other room,' where they could listen without being seen.

There was not much preamble. Captain Evans spoke his credentials and came to the point.

" Christian ! " Alexander West said. " You mean Janet, sir. Christian is my youngest. You mean Janet, or Bathia perhaps."

" No, sir. The mistress Christian."

" It is not credible. Christian is a bairn agin the others. No, no, I will not countenance it. Christian is unversed in the ways of men. It is out of the question, sir. Why, I would not give the child in marriage for a hundred pounds ! "

" I had thought of two hundred," the soft, foreign

voice said, while in the other room they stood rigid in an agony of suspense. "Sterling."

The parents were opposed to an immediate marriage, but Dai was insistent and Christian was willing. The wedding, in the informal Scotch form, took place that afternoon, and that same evening Mistress Evans, in Bathia's new bonnet and Jean's elastic boots, stood on the poop of her husband's ship, the *Dee*, while a fair wind filled the great spread of sail and the couthie little town of Banff, containing all that she knew, receded beyond her horizon. She felt no fear. Only excitement, and a certain satisfaction. She was fully aware of having done a host of rivals well and truly in the eye.

The *Dee* discharged in Aberdeen, loaded a cargo of grain and cattle carcasses, and proceeded to Cardiff without incident save that a fresh quarter breeze, springing up off the Lizard, made the ship lively and occasioned the following entry in the log :

" Mistress Evans is uncommon handy about the ship, even in weather, and would doubtless be of service if a man."

It is not the comment one expects of a bridegroom, but one cannot doubt its sincerity. Dai Evans did not joke. He was an intense and serious man, fiery on occasion yet with his fires subject to his will. His marriage was the one impetuous act of his life, and even in this matter, it will be recalled, he committed himself only after a careful investigation. Prudence appears to have been the key-note to his character, and prudence is a quality which may be known to different men by different names. Give him his due though, he rates more than back-handed praise. He was a good sailor and a good business man, conscientious in all his undertakings yet religious withal. He was masterly at prayers. Moreover—and for this alone we should honour his memory—he kept his log after the fashion of a Pepys and taught Christian to do likewise.

4

From Cardiff the *Dee*, later re-named against all seafaring practice the *Christian Dee*, sailed to Garwyth in Cardigan Bay. This was the home port, Dai Evans's town. He had a house here, a housekeeper, and a family of brothers. The house was big, the housekeeper old, and the brothers hostile save for Thomas, the youngest, who was much too friendly. The town itself was small, go-ahead, and passion-ately Welsh. It closed its ranks automatically against outsiders like Christian. In twenty years' time she might be accepted as one of the townsfolk, but first she must bear her quota of Welshmen and adopt the chapel and the idiom: she must earn the right.

Under these conditions, and with her husband away nine months out of every ten, it is not to be expected that Christian was happy. Her only com-panion was Sarah Ann Griffiths, a disapproving old woman, and deaf to boot; and her essays into the town were punctuated with snubs, and met at best with the kind of cordiality that is bought in shops.

There was no one to admire her new finery, and she would sit on the box-seat at the window overlooking the bay in a gown festooned with ribbons, her hair slicked and her hands clean as a lady's, with nothing better to do than twiddle her thumbs. Sometimes she would weave on her handloom, and then the click and the birr of the pirrin' pin would fill the austere room with a homely and companionable sound. She would write her sister Janet long, passionate letters in which she bared her heart on every aspect of her new life save one; and, tiring, she would sit for hours just staring out to sea where nothing stirred but an occasional white sail and a gull, perhaps, swooping across her field of vision. It was not the life for a spirited girl.

When her husband came home there was bustle and stir in the house. There were guests and elaborate meals. There were social outings and fashionable penny lectures at the chapel hall. There were concerts, and even dances. And above all there were the pleasures which Dai taught her to regard as sinful. It is as unfair to blame Dai Evans for his attitude to sex as it is to blame him for being twenty-seven years older than his wife. Such a gap was, of course, considered not only convenient but ideal in these days when the world belonged exclusively to its males, and similarly, in this age and district, it was taken for granted that a bedding was a dark and violent castigation of sin to be accomplished at the devil's prompting and with all despatch. It must have been provoking to a sensible and healthy woman like Christian, but she does not say so. She accepted her husband as she had accepted her parents. He was hers, to be made the best of. There is no criticism of him in her letters to Janet, and no hint of the intimacies of married life. In all other matters relating to her years in Wales she is voluminously—even tiresomely—informative. We know that in 1847 she spent 11s. on six pairs white silken hose, and in 1848 7s. 5d. on 4 yards Spitalfield glacé silk. We know that in 1850 there were eighteen hoops in her new crinoline, and that she had gone in for something pretty special in the way of petticoats. We know that her brother-in-law, Thomas, smelled of oil of cloves. We know the texts of the sermons that were preached at her, and even the colour of the horses that pulled the various tradesmen's vans. But we haven't the faintest idea what kind of time she had in bed. She couldn't tell Janet because Janet was unmarried. It would not have been proper; and Christian was always proper.

Apart from this one omission the record of her years in Wales is amazingly complete, and it soon becomes clear that she did not yield tamely to the boredom that yawned about her. She girded herself with a pair of diversions, one of them reputable.

She read.

A catalogue of her reading during these years would extend over a dozen closely printed pages, and it must suffice to say that she waded through works as widely divergent as Burton's *Anatomy of Melancholy* and the *Memoirs* of Madame de Staël. She read voraciously, and with increasing acuteness. With the assistance of old Penryn Williams, the minister (of whom she writes to Janet: " He has a prodigious library and, although invariably kind, is nevertheless more interesting and alive than is quite seemly in a man of his cloth "), she mapped and carried through an extensive plan of education.

Her other diversion was less commendable. Discovering the amenities of the cellar, she acquired the habit of tippling. When her husband learned this he was exceedingly displeased, and the next time he went to sea he took her with him.

5

At this time the *Christian Dee* was running to the China Seas, in ballast or with a cargo of light timber and groceries and returning with tea and rice. She had been designed twenty years before for the opium trade and, with a maximum of 8 to 9 knots on a bow-line, was not able to compete successfully with the big Yankee and British clippers which had been built for the job and which had achieved a virtual monopoly of the tea freight. For some time Dai had been contemplating a change over to the South American nitrate trade where the money was less spectacular but the risks infinitely less, and it was only his reluctance to ship a dirty cargo (slate for the Chilean ports) in his inlaid mahogany holds that had so long delayed his decision. Christian's first trip to the China Seas resolved his doubts. He couldn't get out of tea quick enough then.

It is a long run from Ushant to the Formosa Strait. On the outward passage it took the *Christian Dee* anything from 120 to 160 days; and that is a lot of days at sea. If Christian had been merely a passenger she would no doubt have got as bored as was the fashion in captains' wives afloat. But Christian had no intention of becoming a passenger. She meant to be a sailor.

To further this end she made herself as unobtrusive as a woman can ever be on board a ship. She listened demurely to the talk in the saloon where the mate or the second, depending on the watch, joined Dai and herself in a stiff-backed, uncomfortable meal. She stood by the hour on the weather side of the poop watching the hands at work—setting up and rattling down; reeving off new rovings; worming, parcelling, serving; turning braces and halyards end for end; drawing and knotting yarns; reefing, furling, making and trimming sail: the endless seaman's round. She selected the specialists—the sailmaker, the carpenter, and the bosun—and with crisp, calculated questions picked their brains till she had a working knowledge of sails and spars and rigging. Then she turned her attention to navigation. It was something of a joke to the Captain. He couldn't have been more tickled if he had had a talking dog.

At first the weather was exemplary and for weeks the *Christian Dee* bowled along under all plain sail, with an average log of seven knots. She crossed the line on the fifteenth of April, but struck unlucky with her south-east trades, and for four days in latitude 10 south lay all but becalmed while Dai studied the sky warily and fluted his canvas, whistling for a breeze. On the evening of the twenty-ninth small tight clouds began to appear like poised fists in the east, and accordingly both watches were called on deck and sail was shortened.

Next day—the day that the first of the squalls hit

them—George Somerville, the negro cook, was logged ill of smallpox and in considerable pain. By noon the ominous blisters had appeared on the soles of his feet and Dai decided that he must operate. George was a Liverpool negro who affected American manner and accent because he believed that "all classy niggers come from the States." He was a very large man. He had a hammock almost twice the usual size, and before he went sick there had been complaints that he and his berth took up too much room. He was not an easy patient, and when he saw the razor he screamed and turned his face to the bulkhead. He refused point-blank to be touched. He was a good cook and they were anxious to save him. They pointed out that he must have the soles off those feet or die. George said: "All right, suh, I sho chooses to die." They could not persuade him, and they could not coerce him; and when the squall struck they had more important things to attend to, and they left him to die.

Christian, who had been told all the circumstances, herself went forr'd to the fo'c'sle. She measured

George ostentatiously with her arms, then she brought out a bolt of canvas and, squatting on the deck, cut it to size.

"That should serve very well, I think," she said, eyeing George speculatively. "All we need now is a sinker."

The negro watched her with rolling eyes. "I sho don' wanna die!" he said.

Christian produced a Bible and began to read the familiar service to the dead. She had not got very far when he stopped her.

"Tell them they can cut off my feet," he said. "But, missy, tell 'em George sho don't hold with pain."

"The operation will be painless," she promised.

She kept her word. While the *Christian Dee* rolled in the heavy beam sea and the deck above resounded with the clip of men's boots and the thud and scuff of booms and sails, she herself skinned the negro's soles with a razor cauterized over a hurricane lamp, swabbed away the pus, and bandaged the feet. As an anæsthetic she had used a weighted belaying⁄

pin and this, having splintered on the negro's skull, she threw over the side on her way aft to her quarters, "where" (she records) "whether from the buffeting of the sea as we 'hove to' or from reaction, I was for the first time ingloriously sick."

The incident caused a deal of talk on board. Officers and men eyed her with a new respect. She had shown something of her mettle.

The dirty weather continued for six days, then the trades settled in and, crossing the meridian of the Cape in 36 south, they ran close-hauled up a smooth Indian Ocean with light working breezes. The second week in May they reached the first of the islands that sprawl, like spilt pepper, over the charts of the narrow China Seas, and then, in soundings, proceeded with the utmost caution until they finally clewed up with the stately company of tall-masted clipper ships anchored off the Pagoda Rock.

Here, they took in water and provisioned ship, and here, in a series of genteel At Homes afloat, Christian met the ladies of the China Fleet," who," she writes Janet, " despite their happy circumstances without exception bemoan their lot and pine for civilization and the society of nice manners. As this, along with gallantries, comprises their entire conversation, I need hardly tell you that I found them tedious."

Then up the River Min to Foo Chow Foo, that teeming, malodorous river port which owed its wealth and much of its squalor to the illustrious tea of the hinterland. All day long buffalo trains converged on the city, bearing lacquered and enamelled chests of Bohea tea, and sampans similarly laden plied continuously down river to load the ships of the rapacious 'foreign devils' which lay moored in the stream.

It was here, in Foo Chow Foo, that Christian's portrait was painted. The artist was a Mr. Lee, a second mate who had stepped ashore the year the Nanking Treaty opened up the port to trade, and, becoming enamoured of a Chinese lady, deserted and set up house with her in an attic above the Flying Fish Inn, from which point of vantage he could paint the ships that sailed up the Min and, by the simple

expedient of going downstairs, sell the finished articles
to the captains when they called, as they invariably
did, at the saloon below.   The previous year he had
made a tidy job of the *Christian Dee*, and Dai had
therefore no hesitation in entrusting him with the
commission to paint his wife.

It was here, too, and in this same connection, that
Christian first met Tancy McCoy. He cuts a fabu-
lous figure in Clipper history, this Tancy McCoy,
and nowadays it is hard to sift the truth from the
legends that surround him. He is variously described as ' the last of the buccaneers,' ' little better
than a pirate,' 'a wild and dissolute character,' and
' the finest Yankee skipper that ever drove a ship in
sail.'   He had an abundance of friends, and of
enemies ; and I think it likely that his enemies were
handier than his friends with the pen, and that the
account of him which has come down to us has been
distorted by opinions of personal dislike and envy.
Certainly it is undeniable that he was a hard-drinking
and a fighting man, strong in the loin and not over-
scrupulous in the way of business, and it is equally

undeniable that he had salt water in his veins, that he carried canvas to the last and never lost a spar, that the men who sailed with him swore by him and were ready and eager to line up alongside any time he found himself against a wall. Whatever you may think of him you must allow him this: he was a great man in the China Seas by the standards of that time.

Of his appearance at least there is no doubt. Christian, descending the stairs from the painter's attic to the saloon, saw him as " a tall, heavily built man, deeply browned by sun and wind, not ill-favoured yet with a reckless air, his cap on the back of his head, and a look in his eyes which I first took to be merry and half smiled to him in answer, but which I saw then to be most insolent, and could have torn the lips from my face in my chagrin."

" Yes," Tancy McCoy said. " Yes, ma'am, you should always blush. It sure is becoming. Turn around."

She goggled at him and he nodded encouragingly. " Turn around," he said, and before she realized what she was about she had turned. Tancy McCoy had that sort of influence on people. He was an authoritative man. "Yes, *sir*!" he said. "Yes indeed. You're somethin' pretty special for this place. You can knock spots off'n any of the last batch the Swede brought in. I'm Tancy McCoy, an' from now on for a bit I reckon it'll just be you an' me. What's your name, ma'am?"

Christian stood transfixed.

"Whisky!" McCoy said. "Rustle it up, Charlie. And give the little lady her own brand of poison."

At this juncture Dai, who had arranged to meet her at the foot of the stairs, fortunately arrived on the scene, and they left the saloon "to the accompaniment of a braying and guffawing from the louts who lined the bar."

It was not an auspicious meeting. Worse was to follow, for the next day Christian reports: " Captain McCoy raised his hat to me in the street in an exaggerated fashion, which courtesy Dai was forced to return, and I, happening to glance astern, observed that this infamous character had brought about and was following, his hands in his reefer pockets, whistling a mocking air. He entered the Flying Fish close behind us and, on Dai's being engaged in conversation, whispered to me: 'I'll be waitin' for you, babe.' I counselled Dai to be at the bottom of the stairs prompt on twelve noon" (her sittings were from ten to twelve) "and he engaged to be so, but on emerging from the painter's attic at noon, I found Captain McCoy sitting very much at his ease athwart the stairs above the first landing. He motioned me to sit down beside him and addressed me, saying that he wished us to have a little talk. On my disdaining to reply he laughed and told me to take the whalebone out of my corsetry, at which, incensed, I struck him with my clenched fist, simultaneously stepping over his legs and making my escape downstairs. I could still hear him laughing when I joined Dai, but I warrant that I hurt him. The knuckles of my hand are swollen a half-inch. I did not tell my husband of the incident for fear that he would make a scene and inflict some grievous bodily injury on Captain McCoy."

She reckoned that she was rid of McCoy, but she did not know her man.

Two days later, on the occasion of her last sitting, she mounted the artist's dais to find McCoy comfortably ensconced in an arm-chair by the window. She directed a hard glance at the painter and, helpless, he turned the palms of his hands to her.

" Please continue painting," she said.

She ignored McCoy, ignored all his attempts to engage her in conversation. She was pointedly unaware of his presence and at last, exasperated, he struck his fist violently on the arm of his chair. " You rate yourself too high, ma'am," he said. " To the devil with you ! There are growlers enough in the sea. I'll waste no more of my time, but first we'll see if temper'll thaw you. How much is the picture ? "

The painter demurred.

" How much ? " McCoy roared.

" Fifty dollars, but . . ."

" Here, take sixty."

This was too much for Christian. She ran to the

door and called below for Dai, who came at the double just as Tancy McCoy was tucking the portrait under his arm. He caught Dai Evans as he charged, caught him by the throat and held him at arm's length, while Dai's fists flailed unavailingly to reach the big man's body.

"Easy there," McCoy said. "Easy. I'm ready an' willin' to make a widow of her, but are you, sparrow? That's the question, are you?" Without apparent effort he raised Dai off his feet and hurled the Welshman across the attic where he finished on one knee against the wall. Christian ran to him.

Tancy McCoy looked around the room and touched the peak of his cap. "Mornin' all," he said.

Dai got to his feet, brushing his coat, telling the world what he meant to do to McCoy the next time they met. Christian kept her face averted from him and, nettled, he swore volubly in Welsh. "Be reasonable, Chrissie," he said. "A giant like that. What could *I* have done?"

35

" A *gentleman*," she said, " would have drawn his knife."

She could be very cutting at times.

6

They lay in Foo Chow Foo for ten more days, loading a cargo of tea and rice, and overhauling sails and rigging for the race home. In the tea trade speed was the all-important factor, and the big clippers which might be expected to reach England with the first of the new season's tea had their bills of lading signed at £7 per ton as against the modest £2 at which Dai was glad to fill his hold. Nevertheless, like every other captain he refused to admit that any man had the legs of him, and each year his hopes soared anew that this trip would be his lucky one : he would escape a hurricane, he would strike a good monsoon, he would smell out a breeze while his rivals lay becalmed and, running free on brisk westerlies, race through the chops of the Channel with his flying kites set, to arrive first at Tilbury in a welter of glory and fat profits.

It could happen. It was every skipper's dream.

The *Christian Dee* was among the first to complete her loading, and on the eighteenth of June got away to a good start. She picked up a fresh beam wind off Losing Island, but Dai did not like her trim, and would not crowd on canvas. Chests of tea and coils of rope were shifted aft in an attempt to ease her, but still she did not sit to Dai's liking and, on the twenty-ninth, he logs: "Squally sky in the S.W. As she is still tender deemed it unsafe to carry royals and had the yards brought down to deck."

On the thirtieth a sail was sighted on the starboard quarter. She came up fast and was recognized to be the Baltimore clipper, the *Lady Caravel*. She was Tancy McCoy's ship.

Dai Evans immediately ordered both watches on deck. He shook out the reef in his mainsail and set the main topgallant sail. Under this press of canvas the *Christian Dee* bolted along at a spanking rate, but after a little it became clear that the *Lady Caravel* was still gaining.

Everyone was on deck. Everyone was looking to the captain. Dai paced the poop, frowning, pulling at his chin. Finally he gave the order to loose the fore and mizzen topgallant sails.

" That should do it," he said to Christian.

The race was on now in grim earnest. For an hour the *Christian Dee* held her lead, then McCoy set his upper topgallants and again the *Lady Caravel* began to overtake.

" Shall I set the royals, sir? " the mate asked.

" No, no. Too dangerous."

The story of the portrait and the brawl had sped like a cat's-paw through the clipper fleet, and there was not a man aboard the *Christian Dee* who did not know the details of the outrage that McCoy had perpetrated on Mistress Evans. They lined the rail watching with narrowed, hostile eyes as the Yank crept up on the quarter. They did not think the Old Man would let him get away with this. Neither did Christian.

" You've got to set the royals, Dai! " she said.

He ignored her. He was in a towering rage, his

lips twitching as he walked with short, staccato steps from the steering compass to the mizzen rigging.

" He's overtaking fast," the mate said.

" Keep your mouth shut, sir ! "

" Set your royals, Dai! " Christian said sharply.

As if in answer Tancy McCoy loosed his main royal and ran it to the masthead. It was the only answer she got.

" Is it mad he is ? He'll have the spars out of her," Dai said.

Christian gave him a long look, turned on her heel, and went below. Her diary for the day contains a single and apparently unrelated sentence : " I cannot stomach cowardice," she writes.

From her cabin port she saw the *Lady Caravel* come abeam, saw Tancy McCoy brandish her portrait aloft, and imagined she could hear his mocking laugh roll out across the two cables that separated the ships. She slammed the deadlight down over the port and threw herself on her bunk.

An hour later a hand knocked on the cabin door.

" The Cap'n's compliments, Mistress Evans, and you are required on the poop."

" My compliments to the Captain," Christian replied, " and I will come on deck when the royals are set."

The royals were not set.   She did not go on deck.

She did not go on deck for the whole of that passage, and as far as is known she did not address a single word to her husband until the ship docked in Cardiff 127 days later. Then, sweeping to the Garwyth Chapel on Dai's arm, dressed in black velvet shot with orange, an ostrich feather in her hat, she presented the picture of a most gracious and devoted wife, and the *Garwyth Times*, which never failed to comment on the return of a sea-captain, reported that " Captain and Mrs. Evans, who have just returned from the China Seas, are ambassadors singularly well-suited to uphold our national prestige in foreign parts. Granting an interview to our reporter in their handsome bayside residence. . . ." etc.   The rest is also blah.

7

Dai Evans was a jealous and a cautious man. He recognized a red light when he saw it, and as a direct result of this unfortunate voyage decided to cut adrift from the tea trade. For the next four years the *Christian Dee*, refitted, carried slate from the Welsh quarries to the west coast of South America: to Pisagua, Iquique, Tocopilla and Antofagasta, where she loaded the incongruous product of the bleak and sterile Chilean desert: nitrate: nitrate enough to fertilize all the gardens of Wales.

The logs of these years in the west coast, or W.C. trade as they called it, make fascinating reading, and the detailed, day by day account of the long passages round the Horn leaves us with a vivid impression of the problems and hazards that beset the seaman in sail: williwaws, the fierce, heavy squalls of the Straits of Magellan; the vicious easterlies off the Horn, that graveyard of fine ships; the sudden west coast trembler; the terremoto, which flushes the sea into a seething cauldron, hot to touch ; the tidal wave which may lift a ship anchored in twenty fathoms and hurl her half a mile inshore; the physical strain of three—aye, and five months of four hours on and four hours off; the cramped living conditions; the indiscipline (usually in the vicinity of the Line) with the resultant floggings and bad blood; the food—the black bread, the salt junk and harness beef, the rotting potatoes; the diseases—scurvy, yellow and breakbone fever, smallpox, pellagra, beriberi.

It was not much of a life, one would think, for even the rough, tough sea-dog of the day. Yet Christian, a slip of a girl, exulted in it.

At first she occupied herself mainly with navigation. It has been said that navigators are born, not made, and this is largely true, for, though any man can learn to take and read his observation and work his sum from formulæ, it is not one man in a thousand who is correct to a hair's breadth, and not one man in ten thousand who is always correct. But Christian was, and Dai soon stopped laughing at her parlour trick with the sextant. He no longer found it funny. He found it humiliating, and it was a long time before he got used to the uncomfortable idea of his wife's ascendancy. His chagrin was eventually replaced, however, by a genuine pride, for in the summer of 1858 we find him writing in his log: "Mistress Evans fixed the longitude by a snap of Procyon which emerged briefly from a cloud-bank and was not visible for more than three seconds. She has undoubtedly a genius for precise navigation and mathematical calculation, and has devised a method of minimizing error in a position due to error in the observed altitude which, when published, should be of value to all mariners and will bring credit to our name."

Having mastered navigation, Christian turned her attention to the art of sailing, and here too she built on a flair, for right at the outset she had the ' feel of the ship '—that instinctive timing which is the hall-mark of the artist in sail, and the lack of which has cost many a master his spars. On the second trip to the W.C.S.A. her writing appears with unfailing regularity in the scrap log, and from the rotation of hands—the mate's, then the second mate's, then

Christian's—it becomes clear that even at this early stage of her life afloat she had assumed the responsibility of taking a watch at sea.

At the end of the outward passage the second mate deserted. He may have resented Christian's new status. Second mates are notoriously touchy. On the other hand, as by all accounts he was not much of a seaman, and as it had been a grilling voyage, he may merely have decided for an easier life. In any case he deserted the ship at Iquique.

He was not missed. One of the forr'd hands took over his duties aloft and Christian became second mate of the *Christian Dee*, a berth which she filled admirably and which she held until the time of Dai's death.

This melancholy event took place off the Falkland Islands, suddenly, on the 18th of September, 1858. "Dai had," Christian writes, "for some time been suffering from abdominal pains and after breakfast on the morning of the 18th. retired to his bunk with a severe stomach-ache which he attributed to the bad beef. I was standing the forenoon watch and shortly after six bells Mr. Griffiths (the mate) sent for me, saying that the Captain was calling out and in great pain. I straightway went below, but as I entered he was seized with a convulsion of such proportions that it hurled him clean off the bunk on to the deck. While we were raising him his poor body arched like a bow, and when we laid him on his bunk we saw that he had departed."

No sailing ship in the vicinity of the Horn would tempt Providence with so potent a Jonah as a corpse, and that same evening the body was consigned—not without some difficulty—to the deep. It was blowing half a gale, and Christian, finding that her voice would not carry above the skirl of the wind in the ratlines, handed over the Bible to the mate. Twice, at the appropriate stage in the service, the remains, in their weighted shroud, were launched overboard, twice to return as the ship heeled over in a squall so that the corpse, slithering about on the deck, had to be recovered like a hat on a windy day. It seemed foolish to read the service yet a third time and, as if by common consent, all hands fastened on the

unfortunate body and, somewhat out of temper, vigor-
ously despatched it.

Christian thus became owner and assumed command of the *Christian Dee.* She was twenty-seven
years of age, and had been five years and four days at
sea.

8

Iquique, the main nitrate port, was a notorious
eyesore, so ugly that in 1868 even a long-suffering
God could bear the sight no longer and sent an
earthquake to obliterate it. It was a town of wooden
shacks clamped against nature on a slag hill, threatened by sand and sea alike, ankle-deep in bilious,
yellow guano dust, infested with flies, and under
siege from clinkstone and soda sulphate that fell in a
continuous bombardment from the bleak and arid
pampas above. There was no fresh water, no tree, no
blade of grass within a hundred miles. There was no
harbour, no bay even. The ships lay in an open
roadstead with a surf-beat shore, and all loading was
done by lighters from a dilapidated landing-stage.

This was the *Christian Dee*'s destination, and it was here, off Iquique, that Mistress Evans threw her main yards aback and dropped her first anchor since taking over the ship. Immediately the vessel had her chain the touts and boarding-house runners came alongside and, emboldened by the news of the captain's death, boarded her and even swarmed up the rigging to project their high-powered sales-talk at the men still working aloft.

These pimps were dangerous men, and their talk ran to a pattern. " Get wise," they said. " You're being victimized. Now I can get you a berth in a decent ship, big money, a shore job with a woman thrown in, a smart lawyer to sue your skipper, a profitable little business." They had propositions by the score. Englishmen were at a premium in these parts, and there was always a fat commission for a tout with an Englishman to sell.

Christian heard the commotion and came on deck. " Get off my ship !" she said.

They ignored her.

" Thomas," she said to one of the seamen, " fetch

me a musket." With the weapon in her hands she addressed the nearest runner, a swarthy gentleman who was sowing disaffection in the mizzen-mast. " You," she said. " Lay down out of there ! "

He paid no attention.

" This is your last chance. Lay down and get off my ship ! "

" Oh, go to bed with a guano bird," he said over his shoulder, and resumed his hawking.

Christian raised her musket, took careful aim, and fired. The bullet shattered his arm, and his friends, rising like crows at the report, flocked over the side and were gone in a matter of seconds. " I do not regret the incident," Christian writes, " as it was greatly applauded by the crew, some of whom had previously become so restive that I had feared it might be necessary to order a flogging, a measure which I may now postpone, having shown them plainly that I am master and will brook no insubordination."

The nitrate works sympathized with her in her tragic bereavement, and the manager of the *Oficina* himself came off in a boat to offer condolences and, behind her back, a shore billet to the carpenter.

Christian gave him short shrift. She was as suspicious as only a widow can be, and she had discovered that her cargo was underweight. She was in no mood to listen even to reasonable excuses, and she was impervious to Latin-American charm. Granted he had filled the hold, but did he really think she was as green as the stuff he had packed there ! Green. Yes, green as a young tree, and liable on that account to ten per cent. shrinkage on the passage home. She would stand no criticism of her dunnaging or stowing. She demanded that he remove the entire cargo and reload with nitrate, repeat ' nitrate.' The manager could not agree to this. She already had first-quality nitrate. He could not possibly reload. He was sorry but adamant.

" It is deeply regretted, señora."

" It will be much more deeply regretted," Christian said.

That afternoon her boat's crew rowed her to the other ships in the anchorage—a barque, two schooners, and a brig—all Welsh, all nitrate ships. She spoke to their captains and found them sympathetic to her cause—it is doubtful if she would have found them in the slightest degree sympathetic if she had not been an attractive widow—and a common course of action was decided upon.

The following morning a message was received from the *Oficina*, deploring the incredible error and informing Mistress Evans that a special cargo, selected by the management in person and offered at a reduced rate, was ready for loading at her convenience.

In reply Christian despatched a curt note demanding a loading party (an unheard-of luxury) *immediately*. Twenty Chilean rotos were sent out with the lighters and, the manager of the *Oficina* himself supervising, the loading was effected in record time. The widow was mollified, "feeling," she somewhat naïvely comments, "that in the end I had not been unduly imposed upon."

The *Christian Dee*'s last night in Iquique was marked by an incident which, with variations, was to recur several times in Christian's life afloat. She was, it must be remembered, a young and present-able woman, described in Mr. J. D. Munro's book, *Clipper Captains*, as "a singularly attractive girl, with a proud head and sensuous carriage," and even had she been as plain and short-sighted as her sisters she would still, ship-borne, have been the object of desire. She was a woman, and that was enough.

Clifford Griffiths, mate of the *Christian Dee*, was a sober, inoffensive fellow, but the night the loading was completed he fell in with the master and mate of the *Gwinneth Jones,* who were known drinking men. He accompanied them to 'One-thumbed Pete's,' where he was prevailed upon to toast his late captain in a *treepa* of *aquardiente*. The *treepa* emptied, a *chaouch* of fiery *anisardo* was produced to wish Dai God-speed through the celestial shoals, and, by the time this was consumed, along with a few *piscos* for luck, Mr. Griffiths was in a ripe condition, ready for anything.

What actually happened is not too clear. Mr. Griffiths was persuaded—with difficulty, for he was a large and powerful man—to return on board and was bundled into his cabin. Ten minutes later there was a great commotion and the fo'c'sle hands heard Mistress Evans calling out. When they went aft they found her at the foot of the gangway, in night attire and fluttering about in some agitation.

She kept clapping her hands for help. " Steward, steward, come quickly !" she was calling. " There's been a dreadful accident. Mr. Griffiths has hurt himself."

The mate was found lying across the doorway of her cabin, a lump the size of a duck's egg on his forehead.

Little was made of the incident on board, but several months later tongues began to wag when Clancy Vaughan, a sea-lawyer if ever man was, went aft in a mutinous spirit " to git justice, see if I don't " and was served with the same sort of accident, Mistress Evans summoning assistance by clapping her hands and calling excitedly : " Steward, steward, come quickly ! Clancy Vaughan has hurt himself."

The following year, a Swede, a great lady's man on

his own showing, was signed on at Antofagasta. The crew made no attempt to restrain him when he decided on a midnight sortie to the captain's quarters, and he too met with an accident which resulted in his being carried up the gangway feet first. These accidents were all characterized by head injuries and by the manner in which they were announced, Mistress Evans on each occasion dickering about in a very feminine and helpless fashion, clapping her hands for attention and calling: " Steward, steward, come quickly ! There's been a dreadful accident. So-and-so has hurt himself." The order of the words never varied. It was simply the captain's formula, and was respected as such.

Christian herself, as one might expect, has little to say of these misadventures. In a letter to Janet, the first page of which, unfortunately, is missing, she writes, however :

"I sent for him next day" (Mr. Griffiths, obviously) "and, as he had no recollection of the matter, gave him an account of it. The poor fellow was greatly distressed and put about and had some fear, I think, that I might reduce him and send him forr'd to the fo'c'sle. While he was in this frame of mind I took the opportunity of informing him of my decision to make young James Jones, the liveliest hand of the larboard watch, my second mate. Feeling the need for frank conversation, I told him, thus increasing his discomfiture as you may imagine, that I had for some time past noted that he regarded me with admiration and that he had, on occasion, been prone to deal harshly with this or that young seaman whom I had favoured with a smile. I explained—and you will have no difficulty in believing it, dear Janet—that such smiles were administered not as a woman but as a superior, and were as much part of my office as orders to the helmsman. I assured him that, although it had not pleased God that I should return his feelings, I had nevertheless a high regard for his qualities, and I pointed out that he already shared an intimacy with me greater than that enjoyed by any other man. I counselled him, therefore, to be content with his lot, and this he declared himself already to be with so many sincere professions of his respect and loyalty that I am satisfied the matter has been well resolved.

"I fear, Janet, that you may conceive me to have been forward in this, but I would earnestly beg of you to remember that in this life to which I have been called it is not possible, or indeed advisable, always to conform to the ladylike conventions in which we were reared. I have another confession to make, but I will not have it to be sinful, for, as the good Lord has seen fit that I should usurp the functions of my deeply lamented husband, it cannot be unseemly that in the execution of his duty I should appropriate certain insignia of his authority. In any case—and I implore you not to be shocked—I am wearing trousers. I know that Dai would not have countenanced this during his lifetime, but I am confident that he will now have a fuller understanding of the problems that beset the sailor in skirts, and the inconveniences, nay hazards, of petticoats at sea."

At this time of the year—autumn—no voyage round the Horn was ever without incident, and the *Christian Dee*, running before a norther with shortened sail and two men at the wheel, struck a full gale in latitude 50 south and had to be hove to.

For forty-eight hours it blew like scissors and thumb-screws and she would not carry canvas. No sooner was a sail set than it was rent from clew to earing. The mizzen topsail was reduced to ribbons. Stays, shrouds, and halyards parted like cotton. The fore topmast staysail and the main foresail, in shreds, flayed and scourged the air like cats-o'-nine-tails, and the main royal, working loose of its gaskets, streamed out to leeward like a weighted pennant, whipping the mast into a fearful curve as though it had been as slender and as supple as a dowsing rod. The apprentice, a second cousin of the mate, leeched him-self on to the rigging to secure the royal, but was so lashed about the face and arms that he could not hold on, and, blinded, was hurled with such violence to the deck that his leg was broken and his ribs stove in. The chicken-coop, with its precious cargo of poultry, carried away, and the sea that took it was so solid that no one even saw it go. Two new spencers were bent on to the fore and main spencer gaffs and the ship rode to these scraps of sail, taking it green, now standing up on her stern, now lying over almost on her beam ends, tossing and pitching fit to shake the sticks out of her.

Christian did not leave the deck. Muffled in streaming oilskins, protected only by a weather cloth triced up to give a lee, she stood the gale out, nursing the ship's head up to the seas, issuing her orders by megaphone and leaving the binnacle only to lurch to the companionway to consult the barometer, calculate drift, and drink an occasional cup of hot coffee.

On the third day the wind eased somewhat, and, as the glass was rising, she squared away under a little canvas which she was quick to increase, inch by inch, as the opportunity offered. For weeks, after the Cape was rounded, the log shows a hard beat to windward under reefed topsails and fore topmast staysail, then in 25 south, after a spell of variable winds, they picked up the south-east trades, and from then on, apart from a five-day calm in the Doldrums, it was plain sailing with Christian crowding on canvas in accordance with a new sail-plan which entailed a greater press of sail than the old ship had ever known, and under which she bowled along right merrily, rattling out her line like a steamer's. The tide was on the turn as she came abeam Hartland Point, and she raced up the Bristol Channel on the flood.

While the ship was unloading in Barry Docks, Christian, sitting by her open port, overheard a conversation between the carpenter and the gaffer stevedore.

"A woman for Old Man!" the gaffer said. "Holy God, you should be all right."

"I dunno," the carpenter said. "She's skeely, man. I tell you, she's a hard case."

Christian knew then that she had made the grade. Overcome, she hid her hot face in her hands. She even confesses to having wept a little. I doubt if any fashionable beauty ever heard a compliment that pleased her half so well.

9

Dai Evans's affairs were in excellent order. His will was a model of clarity. He left Christian his house, his opium fortune of £27,000—and the pound wasn't to be sneezed at in those days: Christian's father had reared a family on twenty-two per annum —and a half share in the *Christian Dee*. The other half he left to his brothers who assumed quite naturally, this being a matter for men, that they now had control of the ship. They engaged a captain and planned a lucrative programme. Then they approached Christian with an offer to buy out her share. They were very fair. They had no objection to her continuing in partnership if she wished, although they counselled her strongly against such a course. A lady ought not to be directly concerned with trade. It wasn't done. A lady of means had to mind her P's and Q's. They advised her to sell, and they made her a generous offer. It was, they said, much more than her half share was worth.

Christian agreed. "And since that is so, gentle

men," she said, " I believe you will be only too glad
to accept my proposal. For *your* half share I will
give you exactly twice what you have just offered
me for mine."

They were dumbfounded, and when she told
them she meant to sail the ship herself they were
frankly incredulous. They suspected a trick. They
were too sharp and subtle to be easily fooled, and they
saw that she was out to drive a hard bargain. They
raised their offer. Christian, in turn, offered to
double the new price. Baffled, they pleaded, argued,
threatened. They became enmeshed in subtleties,
lapsing into the Welsh language while they haggled
a point among themselves and then, united, turning
to thrust their faces at her, offering concessions which
Christian neither wanted nor understood. Finally
they got very angry. They said things that they
should not have said, and they forbade her the ship.

As a last resort they consulted lawyers. They
were convinced that she was bluffing, and while they
were still putting their heads together, devising com-
promises and stratagems, Christian calmly got on

with the job. She sold the house, signed on a skele-
ton crew, including Mr. Griffiths and the sailmaker,
and on the 14th of May, 1859, sailed out of Garwyth
Bay for the last time, bound for the Moray Firth,
and home.

The family reunion was not as satisfactory as it
might have been, for her father had been dead two
years and a wide gulf of experience now separated
her from her sisters and the friends of her childhood.
She had been away for twelve years. She had
remembered only the good times and now she saw,
with pained surprise, how small and poor her home
was and how narrow were the lives of those confined
to it. It is possible to suspect that even her beloved
Janet disappointed her, and she openly admits that
she was shocked at the sight of her brother Robbie
who, at eighteen, was no taller than a boy of seven.

She remained in Banff for ten days, and during
this time brought her crew up to complement and
entered into contracts on her own terms with Messrs.
Barclay and Adam, Stone Merchants, Aberdeen,
and the North of Scotland Grain Corporation.

She informed her brothers-in-law by letter of her commitments and guaranteed them their share of the profits, then, her dispositions made, sailed once more for South America.

The period that followed was the most arduous and probably the happiest of Christian's life. She was a capable and conscientious captain, and she took a pride in the happiness of her ship. She was strict, but just. Although she was deeply offended by many of the coarser practices of the A.B.s, she nevertheless appreciated that such habits as drunkenness and swearing were the prerogatives of the British seaman and, beyond the advice tendered in her weekly sermons, made no attempt to stamp them out. She herself was a deeply religious woman, and she did her best to encourage the word of God on board by presenting each man who joined the ship with a Bible. But she did not believe in proselytizing, and she did not interfere in any way with her men's private or fo'c'sle lives. Although the *Christian Dee* came to be known as the Quaker Ship, I cannot but think that the jibe was unfair.

On her second trip from Aberdeen, Christian took Robbie with her " in the hope of making a man of him," a venture which, in so far as it entailed stretching him, was wholly unsuccessful, as we find her writing in 1862: " In the two years that he has been with me poor Robbie has not grown a half-inch." He was, however, almost as broad and strong as any of the hands and was well worth his board, not only for his services as steward, but also for his pawky ways and unfailing good humour. He was, it seems, a born clown, and in the long dull spells in the Doldrums, when the pitch melted in the deck-seams and tempers frayed thin, his buffoonery was a diversion and a safety-valve.

Robbie was good for morale. And in particular he was good for Christian, for with him she could occasionally drop the arduous role of 'the Old Man.' She could let down her hair and be a sister. It made a great difference to her to have someone with whom she could talk freely.

The record of the next two and a half years in the South American trade is an interesting and, at times, an exciting one, but no more so, I feel, than that of any sailing ship which habitually cocked a snook at old Cape Stiff. It is not unique, and I am going to skip it.

During this time Christian was carrying granite to Buenos Aires, reloading with assorted merchandise (sometimes of a highly speculative nature : gee-gaws of every kind, candies, gay cotton dresses, beads, etc.) and proceeding round the Horn to Iquique or Anto-fagasta, where she loaded the usual cargo of nitrates for the voyage home.

In the latter part of 1862 circumstances forced a change in this programme. Off the Azores she spoke a homeward-bounder who told her that war had broken out in Chile and that ships were being seized, and when she reached the Argentine she learned that this was true. The Buenos Aires news-papers were full of the Chilean war. Fighting was raging all along the west coast and the nitrate ports were closed.

Here was a pretty pickle. There was no suitable cargo to be picked up in Buenos Aires, and at first

Christian thought of continuing in ballast to China, where she was certain of a cargo. She changed her mind, however, when she happened on an advertisement in the *Herald-News*. It was an advertisement of a bankrupt manufacturer's stock of umbrellas.

" Mr. Griffiths," she said to the mate, " we are going to Australia. The American clippers that used to sail to China in ballast are now calling on the way at Australian ports with general merchandise, and I hear they are making a pretty fortune. We are going to share in that fortune. We are sailing to China, via Australia, Mr. Griffiths. We are shipping a cargo of umbrellas."

" Umbrellas, ma'am ! " (My dear Janet, you should have seen the man's face!)

" Umbrellas," she said firmly. " I know perfectly well that there is not a heavy rainfall in some districts of Australia. Nevertheless, immaterial of weather, the umbrella is a part—indeed an integral part—of the respectable woman's wardrobe. Now, in the mushroom cities that have grown up round the goldfields there must be thousands of women and, I'll warrant, bare an umbrella amongst the lot.   A respectable woman must have an umbrella, Mr. Griffiths. It's a necessity."

"But ma'am, these women are not respectable. They'll never buy your umbrellas. Not the women of the camps, ma'am."

"Mr. Griffiths," she said, "I have read more than you and am therefore, no doubt, a better judge of such persons. All women wish to be respectable, and those unfortunate women who are not respect‚ able wish it most.   I am confident that my umbrellas will be a success."

10

And so to Australia.

The storm sails were set, all top hamper brought down to deck, and everything lashed. The Horn was rounded "with somewhat less than the usual difficulty," and for 6,000 miles the *Christian Dee* ran the easting down, constantly menaced by ice, driven almost to the 60th parallel before favourable winds set in to fetch her up Cook's Strait under a brave show of sail. She reached Melbourne 81 days out from Buenos Aires and arrived, as fate would have it, on the same tide as a black Baltimore clipper—one *Lady Caravel*—captain, Tancy McCoy.

Christian writes: "No sooner had the *Lady Caravel* berthed than Captain McCoy had the auda- city to step on my poop and demand to see me. Robbie brought the message, saying that a handsome American captain wished to pay his respects. I would have been hard put to recognize the gentleman from this description had I not already heard his voice on deck, and I bade Robbie return and inform Captain McCoy that I had nothing to discuss with him either now or on any future occasion, and kindly to serve me by taking himself off my ship. This he refused to do, saying that he insisted on seeing me and *would not budge* until he did. Knowing my man, I thereupon sent for Mr. Griffiths and instructed him to take all hands off the starboard watch and turn the hose on Captain McCoy, washing him off the ship if needs be. This was duly done, despite obstinate resistance on the part of Captain McCoy who even attempted, I am told, to return up the gangway, and was restrained only by the force of the jet which the crew, not without relish, played upon him."

That night, the dockside pubs were full of the affair, and two of Christian's men, returning from shore leave, were beaten up by members of Tancy McCoy's crew. In the morning the ship-chandlers who came on board shook their heads gravely at Christian. They told her that the story was all over town and that Tancy McCoy was a dangerous man to make a fool of. They warned her to be on her guard.

Rumours of McCoy's lurid threats were widely circulated and caused so much uneasiness in the fo'c'sle of the *Christian Dee* that a meeting was convened behind Christian's back, and it was decided that a bodyguard should be formed. This consisted of Mr. Griffiths, the mate, George Somerville, the negro cook (the two most powerful men on board), and, because he insisted, Robbie; and by all accounts this picturesque trio accompanied Christian wherever she went.

It must have been an extraordinary procession: the

handsome, fashionably dressed girl, imperious as any queen; the mate, armed with a revolver; the giant negro, with a belt full of knives which clanked together as he walked; and the grotesque dwarf, with his massive head and shoulders, swaggering, winking and grimacing to spectators, quick as a rattlesnake with his back-chat and ready for any kind of fun.

It is not surprising that this swashbuckling retinue excited a great deal of interest in Melbourne, and that an account of the procession has even found its way into the official annals of the city. Christian herself was fully aware of the stir that she caused and found it, she confided to Janet, "by no means displeasing." Even dealers who did not want her umbrellas appreci-ated the value of a virtue which merited such jealous guarding and treated her with royal respect. Eventu-ally, after ten days' hawking, she found a market for her brollies, and was returning in triumph from the broker's office where the contracts of sale had been signed when she encountered Captain Tancy McCoy, and "as public a humiliation as has ever befallen one of my sex."

Had it not been for a broken shoulder-strap or a defective girdle she would have escaped this unfortunate meeting, for " it was," she writes, " to effect a repair in my costume that I entered the Ship Inn. It was necessary for me to pass through the public room, and this I was in process of doing with averted eyes, as I was conscious of the impropriety of my presence in so masculine a saloon, when a hand grasped my shoulder and, turning, I saw through the haze of tobacco smoke the dissolute and reckless countenance of Captain McCoy."

Events followed fast and furious. Before a single word had been spoken the faithful bodyguard was at Tancy McCoy's throat and the place was in a turmoil. Tables and benches were uprooted. Pictures were torn from the wall. The chandelier was wrenched, in a cloud of plaster, from the ceiling. It was as if a revolving storm was bottled in the room, the vortex an energized mass compounded in equal but indistinguishable parts of Messrs. McCoy, Griffiths, Somerville, and West.

In a few seconds it was all over. Mr. Griffiths lay

by the door nursing a broken jaw. The negro, his skull split open, was stretched out on a bench, as neat as an undertaker's job. And poor Robbie, who had been tossed over the bar-counter, was propped stiff-backed and glassy-eyed against the wall, a sitting target for the bottles toppling from the shelf above.

Tancy McCoy alone of the protagonists was on his feet, but he had not come through unscathed. Both eyes were swollen and he was bleeding profusely from a knife wound in his left arm. He stepped across to Christian where she stood, rigid, by the bar, and, before she could suspect his intention, swept her off her feet and laid her full length on the counter. He held her pinned down with his wounded arm, the blood dripping on to her finery, and with his right hand made a swift exploration of her skirts. He seized an embroidered hem and, ripping a full yard of petticoat off her, threw the flowered silk around his arm and knotted it with his teeth. Then for the first time he looked at her squarely, his eyes merciless and sardonic, measuring her, while the whole room watched and waited.

71

" Your zoo wants tamin', ma'am," he said at last—
that was all—and turned and hammered on the bar
with his fist, calling for a drink.

Christian was no longer a queen. Stripped of her
retinue, her dignity, and her petticoat, she fled back
to the ship like a frightened child. She would have
left Melbourne there and then had it not been that an
opportunity presented itself of scoring off McCoy
whom she had detested before but whom she now
hated, she informs Janet, " with a passion which
smoulders in my heart like red/hot coals, and sets up a
violent throbbing in my temples when I think of him,
and alas, I can think meantime of nothing else but
my degradation at his hands."

It was the second mate who gave her the idea for a
small revenge. " I hear the Chinaman's found a
sucker," he said. " Seems McCoy's going to carry
his corpses, but he's asking a hundred dollars a
coffin, and the Chinaman won't go beyond seventy/
five."

Christian decided there and then.

"Mr. Jones," she said, "fetch me the Chinaman."

The Chinaman was something of a joke. He had come on board shortly after the *Christian Dee*'s arrival in Melbourne and had stated his business. He was, he said, the embarrassed custodian of a large number of bodies. They were the bodies of Chinamen which had been collected from all parts of Australia and entrusted to him to ship home to China for interment in the ancestral burial-grounds. His trouble was that he could not find a ship to accept so unpropitious a cargo. Christian understood that. One corpse was Jonah enough. No sailor in his senses would be shipmate with a hundred. She had shaken her head. " I would sooner ship a crew of Finns," she had said.

Now, however, for the satisfaction of doing Tancy McCoy out of 10,000 dollars she was willing enough to fly in the face of Providence. "I am a religious woman," she said to the Chinaman, " and I respect your faith, although in fact you are no better than a heathen. We must all help each other in this life. I will take your corpses at eighty dollars apiece."

This being agreed, she imposed a condition. " Provided," she said, " they are in good fettle. I will take bones, of course, but as for bodies—I'll take them in good repair only. Is this clearly understood ? "

" Clearly," the Chinaman said. He demurred at the necessity for a receipt, smug with his potted wisdom : " An Englishman's word is as good as his bond."

" No doubt," Christian said. " But I'm Scotch, and a woman forbyes. Here, man, take your paper."

The coffins—most of them highly ornamented— were brought down to the quay and loaded on board. The carpenter prised open the lids and Christian herself examined the contents. One hundred and four passed muster, eighteen were returned to the quay. She indicated them to the Chinaman with a disdainful sweep of her arm.

" Captain McCoy can have these," she said.

II

According to the port records the *Lady Caravel* left Melbourne forty-eight hours later than the *Christian Dee,* yet Christian, when only six days out, reports a race with McCoy, and another humiliation.

The *Lady Caravel* was sighted in the middle of the afternoon.   She was then hull-down on the horizon, and although Christian, with a good beam wind, crowded on every scrap of sail, the *Lady Caravel* continued to overtake, and by the end of the ' last dog ' was in plain view three miles to the southward. She must have been a fine sight as she cut through the blue waters of the Pacific, Old Glory at the masthead, her forecastle awash and her lee rail dipping, a narrow band of gold leaf emphasizing her elegant sheer, the black hull setting off to perfection the great white spars with their reckless spread of canvas—thirty sails in all, fold upon fold immaculate as table linen, gleaming in the evening sun : a Persil ad. in glorious technicolor.

Christian, holding the *Lady Caravel* in her telescope, saw nothing of the Yankee ship's beauty. She was extremely angry, for the crew was looking to her and there was nothing she could do. She was already carrying more canvas than was safe and her masts were creaking ominously. Her best just wasn't good enough. It was a humiliating admission. Tancy McCoy had the legs of her, and soon he would be showing her his heels.

Dusk, limiting the visibility, brought a measure of relief. She could no longer see the *Lady Caravel*, last sighted about a couple of miles on the beam.

" Hand me the telescope," she said to the mate.

" I'm afraid it's broken, ma'am."

She ran her finger over the eyepiece, feeling the ferned surface of broken glass. " That wasn't necessary, Mr. Griffiths," she said coldly. " I can swallow my pills. I do not need to be humoured like a child." For half an hour she walked the poop in a tantrum, as bad-tempered and peevish as only a captain dare be. " Call me if the wind freshens," she said finally, and went below.

Five minutes later she was back on deck. " Mr.

Griffiths," she said, "dowse the lights. We have no choice but to accept the humiliation of being passed, but we can at least deny the *Caravel* the satisfaction of knowing for certain that she has passed us. I want all lights extinguished."

For the remainder of the night the *Christian Dee*, on a taut bowline, sped through a darkness that was unrelieved save for the dim light which filtered on to the compass bowl, and when at last morning came it was seen that she had the ocean to herself. There was no sign of the *Lady Caravel*.

Seven days later they spoke the brig *Carinthia* out of Whampoa bound Adelaide, who informed them that she had seen the *Lady Caravel* the previous day lying becalmed to the northward. Christian received the news with satisfaction and drove on. She had still a chance of showing Tancy McCoy the way up the Straits of Formosa, and she writes that she would have given £1,000 for the pleasure.

Leaving Luzon astern, Christian set course for Formosa but was set inshore and, missing the island altogether, sighted the Chinese mainland north of

Canton. She headed north, hugging the coast; and it was while she was on this leg of her voyage that she had the most remarkable and melo-dramatic experience of all her remarkable life; the experience, in fact, which decided me to write this chronicle.

She was boarded by pirates.

In the early days of the Treaty ports piracy was rife in the China Seas and, with some modifications, still is. The Chinese longshoreman is a born pirate. Beacons, buoys, and other navigational aids habitually disappear, and ships which run aground on the unmarked reefs and shallows are picked bare as a bone overnight.

It was done more dramatically in the nineteenth century. Mirs Bay, where Christian was attacked, was a notorious pirates' lair and to this day, according to the *Chinese Pilot* or *Sailing Directions*, is " littered with the wrecks of looted and stranded ships."

At 11.15, Christian logs rounding the point. " The light airs on which we had been ghosting died away and we found ourselves becalmed in the bay."

Inshore they could see sampans, junks, and lorchas drawn up on the beach, but it was not till dusk when a dozen lorchas put out from the shore that they realized their predicament. Each lorcha contained about twenty men, pulling with long sweeps, and at each masthead was the unmistakable ensign of piracy, a large urn-like contraption known as a stink-pot which, when released by a pulley on to the victim's deck, burst and served as a gas bomb, giving off dense sulphurous fumes.

Christian immediately served out muskets and cutlasses, stationed men in the rigging and on the deck, and herself retired to her cabin with a musket and a pistol. The musket she levelled through the open port; the pistol she laid on the table by her. If the worst came to the worst she intended to shoot herself. She had no illusions about these gentry. They had, she knew, little conception of Western chivalry. When they acquired a white woman they had a habit of holding her for ransom and of returning her, finger by finger, to her friends.

(Christian afterwards advanced a theory that the

pirates had somehow learned of the coffins on board and believed them to be filled with opium. But personally I think it much more likely that they merely recognized the *Christian Dee* as an opium runner and boarded her on spec.)

When the *Christian Dee* opened fire the lorchas separated and closed in from all directions. It was impossible to keep them all at bay, and soon yellow hordes were pouring over the sides of the ship and bloody battle was joined on deck. It would have lasted only a few minutes had a diversion not come from an unexpected quarter, for just then the *Lady Caravel*, moving to a flap of her sails, rounded the point, and immediately fired the Long Tom mounted on her fo'c'sle for precisely such an emergency as this. The defenders took new heart. The *Lady Caravel*, sailing like a witch, nosed up alongside and Tancy McCoy, with a dozen of his men, leapt from her rigging to the deck of the *Christian Dee*. Say what you will against McCoy, by God he could fight! In the brief space of time it took to hack down half a dozen Chinamen the deck was cleared and the enemy, routed, was scrambling pell-mell into his lorchas.

Tancy McCoy tossed his cutlass aside and sheathed his bowie knife. Then he went aft. Christian heard steps on the gangway and knew them immediately to be his. She laid down her smouldering musket and, after a moment's hesitation, concealed the pistol in a locker. When he kicked open the cabin door she was standing stiffly by the table, her face pale and hostile.

" I am indebted to you," she began.

Tancy McCoy closed and bolted the door.

" Save your breath," he said.

She fought him like a tigress, tooth and nail. He on the other hand did not exert himself. Christian tells us that he merely toyed with her. The harder she struggled the better he seemed to liked it. He deliberately let her wear herself out.

" You could always scream ! " he said.

" I fight my own battles," she panted, sinking her teeth into the back of his hand. This appeared to irritate him for, tiring of the play, he pinned her down on the deck, flat on her back, as helpless as a turtle.

"Captain McCoy," she said piteously, "you would not take a woman against her will?"

"Yes, ma'am," he said, mocking her. "If need be."

He kissed her then, and in her private diary she says it was as if he had taken control over her bones, for they bent and softened in his arms.

"Harkee!" he said. "Your friends are comin', ma'am."

She listened and heard voices. McCoy's face, a bare inch from hers, obscured her vision. He was still smiling—leering is the word she uses—and she could feel the heavy pound of his heart against the quick flutter of her own.

There was a knocking on the door. "Mr. Griffiths, ma'am. Do you require anything?" And then, sharply: "Do you want any help, ma'am?"

"No, no. Of course not," she said.

Her diary gives a frank account of the whole affair.

" I could not then meet Captain McCoy's eyes," she writes, " so I closed mine."

Tancy McCoy stayed the night.

Although this was a matter of some consequence in Christian's life it was only of trifling account in the life of the ship, and this she plainly understood. Her entry in the log combines taste with accuracy and reduces the incident, I feel, to its proper level of importance.

" On the night of January 23," she records, " Captain McCoy was accommodated on board."

12

Next morning Christian came to her senses and, making what she describes as a " very feminine and tiresome scene," dismissed Captain McCoy. A light breeze had now sprung up and the ships filled away, McCoy waving and shouting from his deck that he would be waiting for her in Foo Chow Foo. He hoped to perpetuate the relationship. It would have been very convenient, in port. But Christian, a strict Presbyterian, already repented her folly. She could justify a single lapse. After all, she had done her best. She had put up an adequate fight, and had the marks on her to prove it. There was no shame in a yielding to superior force. An acknowledged liaison was a very different matter, and although she had accepted Captain McCoy on this one occasion she had no intention of acquiring him as a habit. She had a nice conception of right and wrong; and accordingly, instead of proceeding to Foo Chow Foo, directed her course to Amoy.

"I shall never," she writes in her diary, "see him again." And the following day she adds an isolated comment. "Never. It would be injudicious."

On the 27th of February she left Amoy with a cargo that consisted mainly of rice and reached Aberdeen four months later to a day: the fastest trip the *Christian Dee* had ever made from China. Christian had then been away from home for more than a year, and it was a year in which a great deal had happened. Her mother and Janet had died of cholera; her booklet, *Aids to Deep Sea Captains*, had been published and cordially received; and her brothers-in-law had at last obtained an injunction restraining her from taking the *Christian Dee* to sea.

For three months, awaiting the hearing of Evans *v.* Evans, Christian cooled her heels in Banff, fretting at her enforced inactivity and writing elaborate memoranda to her lawyer. During this time she designed the house in which she was to spend the remainder of her days and, after careful enquiries, presented the Harbour Trust with the sum of £1,000. In return for this magnificent gift (and at a charge of £3 15*s.* Stg.) she was enrolled as a Burgess of the Royal and Ancient Burgh, a unique honour and one which, a week later, the people of Banff would have given much to rescind.

On the 18th of October, 1863, the case of Evans *v.* Evans came up for judgment, and was argued before Lord Tannadice in Number 3 Court in Edinburgh. It was a dull business. There was only a handful of persons in the court. An elderly Q.C. got up, fiddled with his papers and his wig, and declared without interest that it was intended to prove not only

that a woman was not a fit person to have command
of a ship at sea, but also that this particular woman,
Christian Evans or West, being of a licentious and
promiscuous nature, was *ad hoc* an unfit person to
represent Her Majesty in her trade abroad and to
hold a position of authority over men. It was pro-
posed to call witnesses from Trinity House, from the
Marine Federation, from organizations representing
Seamen's Welfare, and from the crew of the ship, the
Christian Dee.

Christian was taken completely by surprise. She
had not expected Dai's brothers to hit below the belt.
She immediately instructed her counsel to withdraw
her counter-petition and to settle on the Evanses'
terms. Her good name was worth more than a ship
to her : more, I believe, than anything on earth. But,
of course, she did not save it. A lawyer's tongue has
been many a woman's worst enemy. By the time she
arrived, dispirited, in Banff, the tale was in every
house, and children, seeing her step from the stage-
coach, ran excitedly to tell. She was the talk of the
town; an object; the new Burgess, that bitch; a

public shame. The women, who had always suspected her, tore the remnants of her reputation to shreds. It was easy to make money—her way. Well, much good her money'd do her now ! Even her sisters, living comfortably on the annuity she had settled on them, passed her in the street with averted faces.

Christian retired to the big white house on the braes. Here she lived a hermit's life, seen only twice a week when she darted, heavily veiled, to the Kirk. Robbie, alone of her family and friends, remained faithful, but his was not a companionship which sustained her for long, for less than a year after her return to Banff he died 'of the decline,' a phrase which may cover anything from tuberculosis to a broken heart.

Robbie had been the last link with her active and happy life at sea. His death closed the door on her past. There was now no one to recall the old times. No one who knew or cared to know. No means of ever picking up the threads again. No connection whatsoever with that former world. She lived, she writes Mrs. Hartingdon, a London dress-maker, on her memories; and these memories must have had the unreal quality of dreams: her past was so very, so irrevocably dead.

But Christian was still young, and she was rich. It does not come altogether as a surprise to find her marrying again in 1866. Her bridegroom was a Mr. William Buchan, a bachelor of 53, a tailor to trade, and an elder of the Kirk; a very respected man indeed. But, like all of us, he had faults. He had never in his life done anything more athletic than tie up parcels, and he was asthmatic. There is still some record of his speeches at the Deacons' Court and, frankly, they are dull and they are pompous. They are the speeches of a man whose wife has to call him Mr., even in bed.

Christian married him because she was lonely, and because he asked her to; and also, of course, because she liked people to be proper and because, at heart, she was every bit as conventional and respectable as Mr. Buchan himself. Contrary to popular expectations, the marriage appears to have been an unqualified, if not quite a howling, success. The first child, a boy, was born on the 10th of May, 1867.

One morning, in September of the same year, the black, arrogant hull of a strange ship, a Baltimore clipper, was seen to be riding at anchor in the bay; and, later, Captain Tancy McCoy, spruced and nervous, came to pay a call.

At first Christian would not see him, but she had now no crew to throw him off the door-step. Mr. Buchan was at the shop. She had only a scared domestic servant. She made her toilet and went to the door.

She uses a deal of words to describe the meeting. In her diary it stands out like an oasis in the desert of dull, domestic entries.

It got off to an unfortunate start. He frightened her by taking off his cap.

" Captain McCoy," she said, " I'm married."

" You were married before," he said, but his words were incidental only. He was, Christian says, " completely engrossed with looking," and she

89

trembled under the intensity of his stare. He was not a reliable person to be alone with.

"I waited for you in Foo Chow, ma'am," he said. "I waited every year. And then I guessed you must be ill, and I came for you."

"I'm married," she said again.

"Mirs Bay," he said. "I told you then. I told you what I felt. These things, I meant them all. I'm not a man for fine speeches. But what I say I mean, ma'am. Why didn't you come?"

"I don't know. There's no use talking about it. I'm married now, Captain McCoy."

"An old man. They told me in the town."

"That will do. Please go now, Captain McCoy."

"I came for you." He reached out and caught her arm. "Five thousand miles by the log. I'm taking you with me, ma'am."

"Do hush!" she said. "There now, you've wakened the baby!"

She felt him jar under the impact of her words, and she would not meet his eyes. They listened to the baby, who had ceased to whimper and was now bawling lustily.

" He's usually such a good baby too," she said.

He let go her arm, and, smart as a ferret, she jumped back inside and slammed and bolted the door. She was aware of having had a providential escape. She ran upstairs and watched McCoy from her bedroom window.

He stood quite still for several minutes, then he put on his cap and turned away slowly. She watched him till he disappeared round the corner of the brae. She was still trembling. She thanked God, she says, for the baby.

That evening, as she sat opposite Mr. Buchan at her massive mahogany dining-table, the servant came in to announce that two foreign sailors had brought a package. It was large and flat.

Christian retired to her room to open it.

" I saw it was the portrait of me painted years before in Foo Chow Foo." This entry is perhaps the most revealing in her diary. I find it almost unbearable in its pathos. " Even then," she adds, " I did not weep."

13

In the next five years Christian bore Mr. Buchan three more children: two boys and a girl; and after the birth of the last child—the girl—Mr. Buchan, worn out, took to his bed (that massive four-poster in which my own daughter was born) and did not leave it again, alive. Christian did him proud. She gave him a splendid funeral, and a stone which still bears comparison with any in the cemetery. He deserved it all. He had been an exemplary husband and a faithful servant to the community. You could tell his worth from the distance people came to bury him.

Christian's energy was now devoted solely to the task of bringing up her children. Her gifts to the Church and her adherence to clothes at least ten years behind the fashion had to some extent atoned for the follies of her youth. She was not forgiven, but men now lifted their hats to her in the street, and all but a few of the women were prepared to recognize her in passing. She was able to rear her children in ignorance of the cloud that shadowed her life.

They grew up believing that they—and she—were as good as anybody else.

Two of the sons, as one might expect, went to sea, one in the Navy and one with the newly formed Clan line. The youngest son became a minister in Gallo-way and her daughter Janet made an excellent marriage to an Aberdeen physician. Alone again, time hung heavily on Christian's restless hands and, in 1887, with some misgiving at her own audacity, she resuscitated her first love, navigation, and, converting the two big downstairs rooms, opened a School of Navigation.

She did not wish to make money. She wished only to be of service, and her fees were nominal. It was, I suppose, this feature rather than the excellence of her teaching which promoted the school's success. At five shillings a term a mother could afford to take a chance on her son being corrupted, and many of them did. Soon a large wooden signpost indicated not only that the school was established but also that it had acquired the status of an Academy.

Here Christian spent many of what I like to think

were the happiest hours of her life. She taught Navigation and Chart-work, Nautical Astronomy, Trigonometry, and Meteorology, and she taught them well. There are men alive to-day, old men with long memories, who have told me proudly that they sat, as laddies, on Mistress Buchan's long benches, and that there they learned more than just a trade: they learned the nobility of sailing and they learned to love the sea.

The year before her death, as if warned of that event, Christian decided to have her portrait painted. She was not a vain woman, and I cannot but think that her motives were largely moral. She could not bring herself to destroy the Foo Chow portrait, yet she did not wish to be judged by it. She felt it proper to record the other side of the picture. It was her duty to posterity.

On the 12th of December, 1893, at the age of sixty-four, surrounded by her family who had been summoned in good time, she passed away peacefully. She was then almost an institution in Banff, and a whole respectful column of the *Banffshire Journal* is devoted to her obituary. Her death,